THE DAKOTAH GREEN FILES:

MISSION ROBOT

AVERY LUTTRELL

Published by Avery Luttrell through Barnes & Noble
Copyright © 2021 by Avery Luttrell

First edition.

Library of Congress Cataloging-in-Publication Data
Names: Luttrell, Avery, 2006- author.
Title: The Dakotah Green Files: Mission Robot / Avery Luttrell.

Description: First edition. | New York: 2021 Includes bibliographical references

Identifiers: ISBN 9781663572882

Printed in the United States of America

Acknowledgements

A project like this takes a lot of people. Special people that help you along the way.

First, I would like to acknowledge my sister Emma, who gave me numerous ideas and helped me to want to write this book. She edited every chapter to fix grammar and spelling and she cheered me on all along the way.

I would also like to acknowledge my mom. She loved my idea from the start and loved every chapter I wrote. She always knew the right words to put in the book when it didn't sound right. She supported me and helped me to cross the finish line and finish this book. She was one of the biggest, if not the biggest supporter I had when writing this.

My dad was so excited when he heard I was writing a book. He helped in so many ways it is hard to thank him. He took 5 hours editing my entire book and loved every minute of it. He knew what to say and when to say it. My dad has always been there for me and always will be.

I would also like to acknowledge Nonni, Mimi, Papa, GG, and Grampy for reading my book and giving me feedback to help to get me to this point.

Finally, I would like to acknowledge both my dogs Benni and Coco for helping me come up with names for some of my characters.

Dedication

I would like to dedicate this book to my sister and best friend, Emma. You were my first co-author all those years ago. The hours we spent coming up with all those stories was the inspiration behind this project. I hope you see a little bit of you in each of the pages of this book. I could not have finished this book without you and your support. I love you.

Contents

Day: July 22nd

Year: 1950

Place: Earth – in the Future

Prologue

It's a few years after World War II. Many things have changed. If you had the chance, you would have left with the rest of them. I made the biggest sacrifice of my life that fateful day. Now, my family is a distant memory.

My name is Dakotah. Some might say that's a boy's name, but in this time, there is no such thing as boys' names and girls' names. I'm 18 and was born in 1932 in Cincinnati, Ohio. No one around me is human. The beings that are around me are robots that live perfect lives because that's how they were programmed. I am the only human that's left on Earth - and that's not a good place to be.

Day: September 5th

Year: 1938

Place: Earth

Time: After School

It was like any other day at the time. I woke up, got dressed, ate breakfast, and went to school- just as I had every other day prior. My family and I were not the richest, meaning I did not have the best wardrobe to choose from. I had two shirts, three pairs of pants, one dress (for special occasions), and four pairs of mismatching socks. I ate half of an egg for breakfast. Not the most filling but gets me to lunch. Our house is fairly tiny as well. We have a small yellow and white checkered kitchen containing a circular wooden table. There are three chairs surrounding the table - one for each person in my family. Even though the depression hit our family hard, we still managed to get some food on the table. When I walk into the kitchen there is usually a strong smell of coffee as that's what my mom drinks in the morning. When I was eating breakfast, my mom was talking to me about how my little sister needed to be pick her up since my mom could not do it herself. She had to work a bit later than usual.

"You need to pick her up on your way home from school. She is playing with Lizzy when school ends, so can you make sure you can get her there? I'll pick her up from Lizzy's."

"Okay, I understand."

"Thank you."

After that conversation I was out the door on my way to school.

When school ended, I picked up my sister and dropped her off at her friend's house a little later. My sister's name is Poppy. She was named that because when my mom was pregnant with her, all she wanted to eat was lemon poppy seed muffins.

Poppy is only four years old, but she is very smart for her age. She has ginger colored hair, kinda like my mom's. She wears dresses to school and a few bows in her hair. She is skinny, like me, and she shares a room with my mom, as she is too small to share a room with me.

When I got home, I finished my homework and left for my late-night shift at Linda's Market. Our neighbors Mr. and Mrs. Robertson own the neighborhood corner store. I work extra late stocking shelves so we can afford food and clothes. Sometimes I would rather be a cashier. Maybe then I can talk to people…

I finished work that evening at about 9:30 p.m. When I got home my mom was wearing a nice white dress with cherries on it. This is one of her nicest dresses. The dress looks very elegant on her because she has bright red hair that she puts half up and half down. She smells like warm vanilla and orange blossoms, combined with her hair setting lotion. She hates it when she has hair in her face, so the hair lotion keeps it out. My mom has pale skin, and the prettiest red lips. Her lips are naturally red, so she never needed to buy lipstick. I, on the other hand, one day will have to wear lipstick as my pale lips don't compare to her red ones. She is very short compared to the rest of her family. Unfortunately, I got the short genes as well.

"Why are you so dressed up?" I asked.

"I have a date tonight, so I need you to put your sister to bed."

"Okay, enjoy yourself."

Our conversation didn't last long. She was out the door so fast I didn't even get to kiss her goodbye. I was happy she was on a date because she hasn't been on one since dad left.

My dad was a handsome man with bright blue eyes like icicles in winter. He had dark black hair that was always slicked back, and he had a very lean build. He always wore the ugliest khakis with a green and red checkered shirt. I inherited his skinniness and his hair, but that's about it. I have green eyes and very big ears that neither of my parents have. It's something I'm very insecure about but I have to live with it. I also have a lot of freckles on my face and arms. As mentioned before, I am short for my age thanks to my mom. My dad left our family once we lost practically all of our money due to the depression. He never thought he could support us, and he didn't want to be one to make the situation worse. This left my mom, sister, and I to live on our own. My dad loved my sister and I so much, but he couldn't stand looking at our faces knowing he could do nothing to make our lives the best they could ever be. He hasn't written once - even when Poppy and I send letters to him.

I put my sister to bed and listened to the radio. My favorite show was *Joyce Jordan — Girl Interne*. I was listening to it, and when the show ended, I decided to go to bed. This was my normal routine. The next two years would be this same type of "normal", but everything changed once we hit 1941.

Day: January 16th

Year: 1941

Place: Earth

Time: Right After School

It was an ordinary day at school. I went to Science,
then Arithmetic, then English, and Social Studies. In
Social Studies, my teacher announced that the U.S.
was entering World War II and things might change.
I wasn't worried about a family member being sent
off to war because my dad wasn't around anymore,
and my grandpa is too old to fight. When I got home,
my mom was reading a letter that came in a manila
envelope. The letter looked very old, even though
she just received it today. After she was done
reading it, she had the biggest smile on her face.
When I asked her what it was for, she replied,
"They need me in a factory working on airplanes!"

I could tell she was very happy about this because women were not allowed to fight in wars. Later that night we ate dinner which consisted of green beans and a small amount of beef. This is the dinner we usually had because it's hard to afford anything else. For that reason, I never complain, and I remind Poppy to never complain so we don't get in trouble. After dinner I finished my homework, went to Linda's Market, and then came home and headed for bed. When I went to bed that night, I had no idea what the next day had in store for us.

Day: January 17th

Year: 1941

Place: Earth

Time: At Home

As I was coming downstairs for breakfast, my mom was already dressed and ready for her first day at work. She was wearing a bright blue shirt with navy jeans. I had never seen those clothes before, so I assumed that her job gave them to her. Her hair was up in a middle ponytail and she had her blue metal lunch box in her hand that she got for Christmas from my Grampa. I wished her luck and she was off.

I made breakfast for me and my sister. We had an egg with some milk. Same as always. I helped Poppy pack her backpack for school and then I was off. When I got to school, I realized I forgot my homework so I ran home as quickly as I could.

16

When I made it home there was something odd going on. There were a bunch of black cars sitting in my driveway. All of the cars had tinted windows so I couldn't get a good look on the inside of them. I went into the house and my mom was sitting at our kitchen table talking to a bunch of men in black suits. Once my mom noticed me, she asked what I was doing back at home. I replied,

"Today was a day off from school so I came home."

That was a lie, but I wanted to know what all of these men were doing in my house. My mom sent me to my room and told me to do something productive, whatever that means. My room is very small, but I don't complain. It fits my twin sized bed and my small end table which also doubles as a desk. My clothes are hung on a few nails in the wall because my room doesn't have a closet. All the time that I was in my room, I was actually eavesdropping.

I didn't want to make it look that way, so I pretended

to work on schoolwork. As I was listening, I picked

up on a few sentences that didn't really make sense

to me at the time. One of the men in black said, "So

you think you can make them?"

Another added, "It's a hard job to do, you have to be

prepared for the worst."

Lastly one man said, "Good to know that you are

willing to join the effort and make…"

I couldn't hear what he said after that. Once the men

left, I confronted my mom in the kitchen asking,

"Who were those men and what were they asking

you?"

She replied, "They wanted to know if there was a

man in the family that was eligible to fight. I told

them no and they left."

I knew she was lying, and I didn't want her to know I was listening, so I went back to my room to finish the schoolwork I would have done in my classes.

When my mother was about to leave for work, I noticed that she had a totally different outfit on. Today she was wearing a grey jumper with big black combat boots. Big electric gloves were hanging from her waistband. Around her neck she had eye goggles and a necklace. I recognized the necklace; it was one I gave to her for her birthday. The necklace has a picture of our family in it. She never wore it because she never wanted to lose it. When I asked her why she was wearing it, she replied with "Just in case," then she was out the door.

Day: May 21st

Year: 1943

Place: Earth

Time: At Night

It's been a few years since those men first came to our house. They've been here a few more times since then but I couldn't ever figure out why. Each night my mom would come home with oil on her clothes and tiny burn marks that she said came from "resting my arm on the hot metal for the planes." I still never believe her, but I don't wanna push my luck with her. Ever since she took that job, she's been snapping at us more frequently and has a shorter temper, but she also makes more money so we can afford to eat better and have more clothes, so I try not to get on her bad side. So long as it means not eating half an egg every morning for breakfast, I'm okay with it.

As ordinary as it can be, each day for the past two years feels like they have all been roughly the same, other than the occasional troops walking by. I go to school, my mom goes to work, I get home from school, go to work, get home from work, and an hour later my mom gets home.

One major change in our house was that my sister was forced to drop out of school so she could help the boy scouts collect tin to make tanks. The only reason I'm still in school is because I'm the next generation of fighters so the generals want us to be educated. In my free time I teach my sister the basics like how to read and how to multiply. My mom seems to pay less and less attention to our daily activities as each day passes. If something good was to happen to me she wouldn't even talk to me about it. Like yesterday at school - I won the spelling bee, and when I told my mom, she gently said "Nice job, Honey." I could tell she was preoccupied.

She comes home and locks herself in her room crunching numbers and talking to herself. I occasionally go into her room to bring her dinner, but she usually pushes it to the side. She doesn't eat much anymore and it's very noticeable. Her figure has slimmed down quite a bit. This only started when she took up this job. She does reassure me that she eats her lunch and I make her prove it to me by showing me her lunch box in the morning and at night. Her lunchbox usually has a turkey and cheese sandwich with a bottled water and some kind of sweet, so she has sugar in her body.

Day: July 11ᵗʰ

Year: 1943

Place: Earth

Time: Mid-Day

This was a big year for me. I was turning 11 and, in my family, once you turn 11 you get to start purchasing items for yourself like jewelry and nicer dresses. My mom was supposed to take me this Saturday, but she told me she was busy. She and I have dreamed about this day for years. It's supposed to be a big bond between mother and daughter. She told me she had to work on the weekends and because of that she couldn't take me.

She gave me $2.00 and told me that I could buy whatever I wanted. I tried to give the $2.00 back because I didn't want to go without her, but she told me to go because she may not have an open weekend until the end of the war. After she forced me to take the money, I decided to take my sister to go buy something for her. Poppy seemed so happy; she hasn't looked that happy since she was at school with her friends. She misses being at school. I can tell. Once we got home, she put on a show to model all the clothes she got. It was fun but deep down inside me I wished that was me modeling for mom.

Once my mom got home, I made her dinner, and once again she pushed it off to the side and didn't eat it. After she went to bed I snuck into her room and tried to figure out why she seemed so stressed lately. All I could find were broken screws and sketches of men, women, and children's bodies. I left her room in a hurry because I heard footsteps. Turned out to be Poppy. I couldn't stop thinking about what those papers could have meant so I quickly ran back into her room, grabbed one of the sketches and ran out. I wanted to study the page more to figure out what it was for.

The next day she didn't notice that the paper was gone so I didn't say anything about it. She left for work in a rush. I knew she left in a rush because she left her coffee at home and she *NEVER* does that. Apparently today she needed to get to work early because "Something big was going to happen!" I didn't know what it could possibly be because she claimed she was working on aircrafts and those that have been in flight since 1903.

Day: July 13th

Year: 1943

Place: Earth

Time: A Few Days Later at School

I was sitting with my friends at a school lunch table and we were talking like we usually do. The lunchroom is smaller compared to other school's lunchrooms. There are lots of dust bunnies in the corners of the room and the walls were the standard white and blue. The lunch tables were circular, and we had to sit in tiny wooden chairs which were very uncomfortable. I have four friends, Sarah, Savana, Susan, and Silvia. We are known as the "4 S's and a D". We were inseparable.

Sarah has brown hair and glasses. She is very tall and has a funky personality. She enjoys listening to the radio and playing board games with her family.

Savana tries to be popular, so she hangs out with the richer group. She doesn't think we know, but we do. She has wavy blond hair and is also very tall.

Susan has black hair like me. She is very sarcastic and loves all animals. She is not short, but she is not tall either, so we consider her the middle ground of the group.

Finally, Silvia. She is a year younger than us, but she is extremely smart, so the school moved her up a grade. She has a shy personality and long brunette hair. She has a round face and a small nose where her glasses rest. She also wears the same ugly pea green color to school every day because she thinks the color looks great.

As my friends and I were talking, Sarah started to say, "I heard for World War II the Government is making…"

Savana cuts her off saying nobody our age cares about the war. She then proceeded to talk about her cherry lip-gloss she just bought. We never heard what Sarah was going to say. Throughout the day I wondered what it was that she wanted to talk about because I was interested to know if it had anything to do with the sketches I found in my mom's room.

At the end of the school day, I walked up to Sarah and asked her what she was talking about at lunch. She quickly answered, "I heard that the Government is hiring people to make robot spies, so nobody actually gets hurt and we get information. Of course, this isn't real because…"

She never finished her sentence because her mom was calling her over to go home. As they were walking away, I noticed that Sarah's mom was wearing the exact same outfit my mom leaves in every morning. I packed that image in the back of my mind and walked home, although I walked much slower than usual because I was wondering, "Was what Sarah said true?" My mom has a bunch of sketches of human bodies. Could that be what she had them for?"

Of course, I would never know because what Sarah was saying most likely was not true. Or so I thought.

My mom came home around the same time as usual

and sat in our living room. Our living room is one of

the biggest rooms in our house. It has a comfy grey

couch from so much wear and tear and a bright

purple Pelican chair known for its curvy shape. We

found the chair at a rummage sale and we needed

something else to fill the empty space. When my dad

lived with us, just a couch wasn't cutting it, so he

bought the purple chair. There is also a small

wooden table that has our Philco radio on it. My

mom chooses to sit in the chair for about 10 minutes.

After that, she generally goes straight to the

bathroom where she washes up, and then heads to

her room. Knowing this routine, I hatched a plan. After she washed up, I was going to block the entrance to her room and confront her to figure out what she was actually doing.

As expected, she got up and went to the bathroom. Our bathroom is very tiny. It has a sink, toilet, and shower. It is all white other than the striped pink and blue shower curtain. I listened for the shower to end. I waited to hear the three drips the shower gives once it's off. Those drips counted down the seconds until the confrontation. I heard the lock on the door click, sending a shiver down my spine because I knew what was about to go down.

I witnessed the door handle turn. At that moment all of the adrenaline coursing through my veins startled me. All that adrenaline was like a bomb waiting to detonate. The bomb was lit, and I ran as fast as my tiny legs could bring me. I ran. And ran. And ran. I was in the living room which was down the hall of the bathroom. I needed to get there before my mom got to her room. As I ran, I felt something inside me. I didn't know what it was, the guilt I might have after, or the adrenaline running through me, or was it the pit feeling in my stomach because I was nervous for what my mom might say to me. I didn't know whether she was going to lie to me again or if what Sarah was saying was true. Either way, I needed to get to that door.

Day: July 13th

Year: 1943

Place: Earth

Time: Minutes Later

I make it to the doorway just in time. My mom jabbed me in the arm as she was reaching for the door handle to her room which was located right next to the bathroom.

"What are you doing, Dakotah. Let me into my room."

"I won't move until you tell me the truth!"

"What are you talking about?"

"I want to know what you are actually doing when you lie and say you are working on building planes!"

"Where are you getting all of this from. I don't lie to you."

I knew she was lying to my face.

"Mom I know you don't go build planes because the first day those men in black suits were here, I was eavesdropping, and I heard some of what they were saying. I didn't hear most, but I know they were not talking about planes."

"DAKOTAH TOBYN GREEN! Why were you listening? I have taught you better than to do that!"

She was getting mad, but I wasn't going to leave without answers.

"Mom stop avoiding the question. What do you actually do when you go to work? I know it's not building planes because when you were sleeping the other night I snuck into your room and found sketches of human bodies. Why do you have those? I want an answer so don't avoid the question."

My mom was beginning to calm down. She said to me, "Dakotah it's not right to go through people's stuff especially your parents. I need you to come and sit down because I think it's time, we had a chat."

She sat me down and we had a long talk and I couldn't believe what I was hearing. She told me that some people from the government came to our house that day when I told her I didn't have school to talk about a special assignment. On the first day of her job, she told me that there were scouts looking for people who could potentially do a particular job. Her and nine other women (including Sarah's mom) were chosen to create Robots - machines that gather intel from the other side.

"So like spies?" I asked.

"Yeah like spies. The reason for this is so that if the enemy figures out that they aren't human, no real people get hurt."

This seemed valid but it still didn't connect to all the body sketches and the broken screws. When I asked about both of these, she replied, "The screws were from parts that didn't fit or that were broken so I took them home to try to calculate the size we needed. The sketches were made so we could get proportions right in order to make them look real."

She continued talking but started to use hard math terms that I didn't know so I didn't understand what she was saying. Eventually she told me she was missing a sketch, but I couldn't bring myself to tell her I took it, so I said that I didn't know where it was.

"Do you understand now?"

"I understand."

I said I understood, but in reality, it was hard to process all the information at once. That night I laid awake because I couldn't go to sleep thinking about the fact that my mom was making robots for the government.

The next morning my mom left me a note on the counter saying:

"Please pick up milk from the market on your way

home. Thanks! -Mom"

I ate sausage and eggs for breakfast this morning. It's nice to eat food that's not just half an egg. As I was walking to school, I wondered whether Sarah knew all the details about her mom's job as well. All I knew was that I was not going to be the person to tell her.

Day: June 6th

Year: 1944

Place: Earth

Time: At Night

I went through all my classes wondering about what my mom could be doing at that exact moment. After school ended, I picked up the milk and went home. I cooked some dinner for the Poppy and I. Tonight, I made a canned ham on the stove. It smelled like heaven. At least it does when you are used to green beans and small amounts of beef. After dinner, I taught my sister a lesson on multiplication and let her go to her room to play. I turned on the radio because I had a little extra time before heading to Linda's. The radio was packed with soap operas and news on the war. The announcer was talking about how the U.S. troops had just invaded Normandy. I thought that the segment was very interesting, but I had to leave for work in the middle of it.

Later that evening, while I was at work and stocking shelves, I noticed three men in black suits looking at the canned goods. They seemed to follow me around the store pretending to look at different items, occasionally picking up one or two. Eventually, I built up enough courage to go speak to them and ask them If they needed anything in particular.

"Hello, is there anything I can help you find? Meat, canned peaches, green beans, potatoes?"

One of the men responded with, "We need to talk. Not here, not now, but we need to talk."

With that they left. I didn't stop them because I didn't know what to say. When my shift ended, I left work and went home.

As I entered the house, my mom was sitting on the couch. She's never home when I come home from work. She looked like she was waiting for someone. I knew it wasn't me because she told me I should go to bed early. I did what she said and went to my room. I knew deep down that I shouldn't wait for someone to show up and if or when they do, I shouldn't listen to their conversation.

A half an hour later I heard someone knock on our front door. I cracked open my bedroom door ever so slightly to see who it was. My room directly faces the front door. I saw a tall gentleman in a black suit standing in the doorway. My mom led him to the living room. I couldn't see into the living room, so I just had to listen. The man in black started talking to my mom.

"We have an issue. All of our adult robots 's are doing great, they are looking and functioning like they should. The children, on the other hand, are not doing as good. We can't figure out why. All the same people are working on these bots and the children just don't seem like today's kids. They don't act the same. We think that the only way for them to act right is to add a kid to our team." He continued talking, "We have looked at all the kids in the local school and their potential along with their grades and we think the best fit for this position is your daughter, Dakotah. Will you consider her working for us? She only has to work on the weekends."

My mom didn't even get a moment to think before the man in black added, "We will give you three days to think it over. Just know that if you let your daughter work for us, you will be greatly helping your country."

He didn't give my mom any time to reply, stood up, and walked out the door in silence. I didn't even know how to reply.

I stayed up an hour after the conversation because my mind would not rest. I couldn't believe the government was interested in me - out of all people to work on their bots. I kinda felt nauseous because I thought back to when my mom was talking to the men the first time. One of the men mentioned "…you have to prepare for the worst." I don't know what the "worst" is, but looking back, I definitely wasn't prepared for it.

Day: June 7th

Year: 1944

Place: Earth

Time: The Next Day

When I was getting ready for school the next morning, I was still processing the news. I technically wasn't supposed to know about the job, so I didn't bring it up at breakfast. I anxiously awaited (in the wooden chair at our kitchen table) for my mom to bring it up. She never did. She made some ham leftover from last night's dinner and eggs for breakfast and left for work.

When I made it to school, I slyly asked Sarah some new questions, but she still didn't seem to know about her mom's job. While I was sitting in math class learning about 3D shapes, the loudspeaker blared a message, promptly waking up the kid asleep in the back. The voice over the speaker said, "Will Dakotah Green please come to the office and bring all of her belongings."

As I was grabbing my grey notebook from my desk and heading to my locker, I wondered why I was getting picked up because mom didn't tell me she was picking me up early.

I made it to my locker and I spun the lock to the little tune I made up to remember my code, "spin the lock 3 times to the right, go to number 29, spin the lock once to the left, go to number 33, finally go straight to number 42." Once I opened my locker, I packed my things in my plain forest green backpack and headed to the office.

I never liked going to the office because the receptionist had giant glasses and was very old. She smelled of cloves and nutmeg. Her hair was as grey as the sky before a storm and she always had the longest fingernails that she painted red. She talked in a very nasally voice and was quite intimidating. As I arrived at the office, I realized something. My mom wasn't picking me up. A man in a black suit was standing there waiting for me. He looked me in my eyes and said, "We have to go now!"

I followed him out the door and wondered why the receptionist didn't ask how we knew each other.

Day: June 7th

Year: 1944

Place: Earth

Time: In the Car and the Factory

I followed the man back to his car, which was also
black. I recognized him from the market the other
night. He was the man that told me we needed to
talk. Maybe now is the time.

He opened up the door for me and indicated
that I should sit in the back seat. His car was very
nice. It has grey leather seats with grey carpeting,
and beautifully polished leather doors. There was
also a sunroof that looked like it had been sealed
shut. As the man got into the car, I was able to get a
better look at him. He had dark brown hair with a
mustache and was wearing the same black suit as the
others I had seen. Interestingly enough, he had one

of his ears pierced with a gold hoop. He was pretty tall and looked as if he had a medium build. After he started driving, I asked him, "Who exactly are you and where are you taking me?"

He responded by saying, "I'm not allowed to say who I am for security purposes, but I am taking you to a secret facility because you have been hired as a robot maker."

I didn't know how to respond because my mom had already told me about the project, so I knew what there was to know.

We drove for what felt like around 30 minutes. Once we came to a stop, the man turned around from the front seat and handed me a blindfold. He told me I needed to cover my eyes because they didn't want me to know where the facility was located. I didn't argue with him, but I was concerned that this was all a hoax and in reality, I was getting kidnapped. I put the blindfold on, and he led me to what he described as a doorway.

For some reason I wasn't scared. Maybe it was because my mom knew these men or maybe it was because I was to naive to be scared. I was more confused than anything.

As the blindfold was slowly lifted off, I could start to see a door that was grey - just like the stone wall it was hanging from. The man pulled out his badge and swiped it through the security pad. With that, the door clicked open. I walked inside with amazement. There were conveyor belts all around, each with a different robot part on it. I could see hands and legs headed in all directions. The strange thing was that they looked just like human hands and legs. There was a heavy smell of oil and not many people in the building. After a minute of staring in wonder, the man said to me, "Amazi'n inn'it. Once we figured out how the adults were put together and everything they needed, we were able to mass produce everything. Instead of taking three hours on one robot we can make 25 robots in three hours."

I was staring in wonder. I was also curious if they could figure out how to mass produce adults, how could they not figure out how to mass produce children?

Eventually the man led me to a room with a glass table and a bunch of glass chairs around it. Another man dressed in black sat in one of the chairs, while my mom sat in a different chair next to him. I was directed to sit in the chair directly across from my mom. The man in black started the conversation by saying, "I know this might seem weird to you, but we need you here. My name is General Calcut. As you might be able to tell, we make robots in this warehouse. These robots are sent to other countries to collect information for war purposes."

General Calcut was a younger man. He was extremely skinny and had blond hair. He had a very squeaky voice, and so, at times, it was hard to hear what he was saying.

"If the other countries figure out that they are spying for us, the robots are able to self-destruct, so they don't get our information or our technology ideas. We have our adult bots down pat. That's why we are mass producing them. Our children bots, on the other hand, are not going so well. They don't act like children; they act more like broken robots trying to be a human child. For this reason, we asked you to come in here to help us get these children bots right so we can mass produce them. Your mom has already said you could work here, but we still needed your thoughts on it."

I could tell he was waiting for a response from me, but I didn't know what to say. Even though I knew this day was coming, I still hadn't prepared an answer. I ended up confidently responding, "If this is the only way I can help our country, then sign me up."

My mom's face lit up. I could tell she was happy with my answer. The Generals face also lit up, so I knew I made the right decision. The General ended our conversation by saying, "We thank you and the country would thank you too if they knew. You will need to arrive here at exactly 8:00 a.m. sharp with you mom tomorrow morning. From this point forward you are not going back to school.

When you get here, you will get all the information

you need to know."

As we finished our conversation, I was

escorted out of the building and dropped off at home.

I had to think about what had just happened.

Day: June 7th

Year: 1944

Place: Earth

Time: Later that Night

It became clear that I was not going to be able to concentrate on my homework as my mind continued to wander. But then I realized I didn't have to worry about homework anymore.

I knew about the plan, but I didn't know my mom would say yes and that it would actually happen. When I was sitting on the couch, my sister walked up to me and asked, "Where were you tonight? You were supposed to make dinner. I had to cook up some eggs which were burnt."

In all the chaos, I totally forgot that I was supposed to make dinner tonight.

"Sorry. I just got caught up in…" I had to choose my words wisely because she couldn't know what was happening. "... a study group for school. Tell you what, to make it up to you, we can play whatever you want to play until you have to go to bed. OK?"

"OK."

For the rest of the night we played together until I had to put Poppy to bed. At that point, I patiently waited for my mom to come home so I could talk to her. Uncharacteristically, she didn't come home around the time she usually does. An hour had passed, and she still wasn't home.

While I was waiting for her to get home, I started to write down a list of questions I had for her. When I was done with that, I sat in the purple chair in our living room, listening to the radio. The radio we owned was brown and small. We couldn't afford a nicer one because we didn't have a lot of money.

As time passed, the radio got boring, so I turned it off and started to read. I was in the middle of a book called _Gone With The Wind,_ when the front door suddenly swung open. My mom entered the house like she had done a thousand times before. When she saw me sitting up waiting for her, she asked, "Why are you still up?" Then she asked, "What do you want to know? She knew why I was up, and she knew I had tons of questions.

I quickly pulled out my list and fired off the first one, "Why did you let me do this?" She responded, "Because I knew it was right for the country and they wanted YOU!" I then asked, "How come they only want one kid when they have ten adults?" to which she answered,

55

"They didn't want a lot of kids because they didn't want to have the secret spread. Kids talk more than parents."

The questions I had lasted for a good hour. Finally, all my questions had been answered and I was happy that all of this was cleared up. My mom sent me to bed and told me to be ready for what I had to do tomorrow.

Day: June 8th

Year: 1944

Place: Earth

Time: The Next Day at Work

This morning, my mom came into my room bright and early to wake me up because we had to leave soon. She told me they had a uniform at the warehouse waiting for me, so they didn't care what I showed up in. As she was cooking up breakfast, she was telling me that we had to drop my sister off at Lizzy's house because we were going to be gone all day. I had to eat fast because mom was practically out the door as I got my food.

Once we dropped Poppy off, we headed straight to the warehouse. This time I could see where it was because my mom didn't blindfold me. I had seen that place before, but our teachers had warned us not to go in there, so we never did. My mom pulled out her special badge and swiped us in. I secretly hoped I would get a badge soon.

As soon as we stepped through the doorway, we were greeted by a bunch of people - all in black suits. If you looked in the back you could see a bunch of workers already working, each dressed exactly like my mom.

I was taken by one of the men in black to a different room as my mom started working. They gave me my outfit which was pretty much the same as my mom's just in a smaller size. Once I had changed clothes, the same man sat me down in front of a white screen and took a photo for my badge. He told me that the badge should be ready in the next 4 to 5 business days. Another man then escorted me to a room where General Calcut was sitting. General

Calcut started to talk to me. He said, "I'm glad you're here. You made the right decision to help your country. In just a few moments you will be taken to a room where some people are going to take measurements of you, and have you taken some tests to make sure you will be able to do what we need you to."

When he was done talking, one of the men in black that was standing around the room grabbed my arm and led me to a different room. Here a nice lady dressed in a white outfit started to take measurements of my body. She had a kind face but was serious. They wanted to make sure that their children's measurements were similar to those of a child. She had a very long measuring tool that she would put up to each part of my body. When I was done, she would take that measurement and scribble it down on a piece of paper. This process went on for another hour. When she was done measuring me, she told me that this is very helpful because a lot of their measurements were way off.

Just like General Calcut said, I was then escorted to a different room where a different man was standing. He sat me down in a chair that was connected to a desk and handed me a piece of paper. There were a bunch of math problems on it. I enjoyed math, so a lot of the questions on this paper were very easy for me. I finished the first test in 20 minutes and was immediately handed a second test. As quickly as I finished one test and I was handed another. This would go on for another two and a half hours.

When I was done with all the tests, the man standing in the room took the stack of papers over to a machine where he would scan them to ensure that I had answered correctly. After the machine he looked at the tests and looked puzzled. Then a few minutes later another man came into the room. Both of them went through all of the tests a second time. They appeared amazed. The man that gave me the tests told me that all of my answers were correct and that it was insane that I managed to do that. He explained to me no child or adult managed to get perfect scores on all of those assessments like I did. He told me I was one of a kind. I felt proud of myself, but my brain was fried from all the math problems.

General Calcut didn't tell me what was going to happen next, so I was surprised when I was brought to a part of the factory where a bunch of robots were standing. The man that brought me there told me that I was going to start working on robots immediately. I was shocked that they wanted me to start so soon. I barely knew what I was doing.

I received a quick introduction on how each robot part was supposed to fit and how the robot was supposed to look. Based on the new measurements, they managed to create a few parts that would make three robots. I just had to figure out what type of screws that had to be used, and where they would need to go. It took a couple of minutes, but I figured that out relatively quickly and started to assemble the robot. As I completed the first robot, I sat it off to the side.

I started to assemble robots and experimented by using different types of screws for each part. It took me about four hours to figure out exactly what parts needed to be attached by what screws. I assembled the robot completely and put it off to the side so that I could start on the next one. As soon as I moved this robot, an older woman frantically ran up to me and started yelling at me. She said, "WHAT ARE YOU DOING?!" to which I responded, "Working on robots. I finished that one, so I put it off to the side."

"YOU CAN'T DO THAT! YOU WILL GET YELLED AT!"

She then picked up my robot and took it to one of the men guarding the doors. I wasn't able to hear what she was saying but she looked like she was trying to tell the man something important. After she finished talking to the man, a voice over the loudspeaker announced that the lady had figured out how to make a child robot.

I didn't really know what to say because I knew inside that I was the one that figured it out, but no one else knew that. No one asked her how she figured it out. I must have been super mad because as people were congratulating and cheering for her, I approached her and asked her how she figured it out and what type of screws were needed to assemble each part. I knew she didn't know the answers to my question when she didn't respond.

To prove my point, I picked up my notebook where I had everything written down and showed everyone congratulating her that I knew exactly how to put together the child. Upon hearing this, one of the men in black quickly escorted her out of the room and I didn't see her the rest of the day. I kind of felt bad but I didn't want someone taking credit for something I had done.

By the end of the day I had completed 8 robots and was extremely tired. I was instructed to go to General Calcut's office and tell him what I'd figure out. After we spoke, he told me that the robot parts with the new measurements would not be in for another four to six days.

My mom came and picked me up from his office and we drove home. She was very proud of me. I went straight to bed as I was extremely tired. I felt very accomplished with how my day went and I was excited to go back.

Day: December 17th

Year: 1944

Place: Earth

Time: At Work

It has been a few months since my first day and many things have changed. I no longer attend school. I'm working every day at the factory with my mom. I can now make ten robots per day and I have recruited some people to help me to make more. Making the children bots is now a job for me, Ko-Ko, and Benny. Finally, two people my own age.

Benny is a free spirit. He doesn't really do much to help but I need him because he helps with the male robots. He has dark black hair, a circular face, and glasses. His skin is so pale, it almost looks like fresh fallen snow. He is very mathematically smart, but he doesn't ever want to admit it.

Ko-Ko is very hard working. When added to my robot count, we create twenty-two robots a day. Ko-Ko can make them faster than me because her hands move at a quicker pace than mine. Ko-Ko is fairly short, she has extremely short curly brown hair that shimmers in the sunlight, she also has gorgeous eyes. Her right eye is like an ocean wave that glistens when you look out your bedroom window at the beach. The other eye is like green murky water that usually has fun creatures in it. Her mismatched eyes are what make her unique. Her skin is the color of cocoa.

All of us work well together and we are extremely excited for tomorrow as the first batch of robots are being shipped off to Germany. These robots include the robots that I've made!

The robots look like real humans. You can't see the screws and bolts because those are covered by Nazi uniforms (we want them to look as real as possible). They don't act the way movies portray robots acting. If you didn't know they were made in a factory, you would never know they were robots. All of that is thanks to our amazing programming crew. The robots are able to speak 124 languages so they can go most anywhere and understand what the people are saying. The robots also have little cameras in their eyes so we can see what they see. The cameras record what they see in case we need to look back on it.

There are exactly forty robots going overseas and sixteen of them are mine. My only wish is that this goes well, because if the Germans figure out that we are using robots to spy, this could potentially be disastrous for us.

The robots were made to spy, collect information, and bring it back to us so we would know how to end the war. Everyone in the factory is anxiously waiting for tomorrow hoping nothing goes wrong. If one screw is loose or the clothes are not exactly right, it could mean something bad for the U.S.

Day: December 18ᵗʰ

Year: 1944

Place: Earth

Time: The Next Day

Today's the day, and I am extremely nervous. There were so many 'What If's' that could either make or break the entire afternoon/evening. Mom made toast with jam for breakfast. I didn't eat much because I was too nervous for what was ahead. The time had finally come… to leave for work.

When we got to the factory, nobody was working like when we usually get there, everyone was sitting at their workspace doing nothing. As I walked to my desk, I noticed that Ko-Ko and Benny were already there. I asked them why nobody was working, and they said that General Calcut had an announcement that they were waiting for.

A few moments passed and General Calcut came out. He started with,

"Today is a very nerve-racking day indeed. I am very proud of how many robots that have been made thus far. Even though we are sending out forty of them today, we can't stop working. Today at 10:30 a.m., the robots should be ready to be shipped out. At 10:20 a.m., I want you all in the big office so we can watch them board the ship and see the ship off! Thank you for your time - now get back to work"

We all pretended to work, and as you can imagine, not a lot of progress was made because all we could do was think about how this could go wrong. From the time that we arrived at work until 10:15 a.m., I assembled only two robots. That's not a lot but it's more than some people.

10:20 a.m. hit and we all marched upstairs. I could hear little bits of conversations from the whispering, but I didn't want to listen because most people were saying what if one of the robots broke down. We all crammed into the big room. There were enough chairs for everyone. I sat in the front - seeing that I was short and would never be able to see behind some of the adults. General Calcut told us that this was the day we were all working for and all of us needed to be here to watch it happen. He flicked on the small television screen and we all gathered around. The screen read:

10:32 a.m.

Mila Weber

Nurse

It was kinda cool that it showed us who we were looking at and what they were sent out to do.

We watched the robots walk through back alleys. They had to walk through back alleys because they were dressed in Nazi uniforms and we didn't want to scare the people. The robots walked closer and closer to the boat and the tension in the room grew. Finally, the boat was in sight. The robots boarded the boat and that was it. All our work was now headed overseas.

Once the robots were safely on the boat, we were told that there was a surprise. Because of all of the work we had done, we were each given a small television to watch our specific robots. I got a television that I was to share with Benny and Ko-Ko because we were working together. I had mixed emotions about everything that was happening. I was happy that my robots were shipped off, but I was afraid that there was a miscalculation and some of them would malfunction- compromising the mission.

I left the room and started work again.

Day: December 22nd

Year: 1944

Place: Earth

Time: Work

For the past few days, I've felt that work has been getting worse. General Calcut doesn't come out of his office and talk about what we need to do better and what looks good. He is glued to the screen watching everything the robots are seeing. I see my mom less and less. The General has her working double as one lady got really sick and couldn't come into work. Because of that, my mom has had more stress than ever before.

All she talks about (to me of course) is how she needs to make more robots and how she needs more help because none of the other women want to take on more than they have to. She doesn't take a lunch break anymore, so in any free time I have, I walk over to her and make her stop working so she can eat some food. My mom and I come home later more frequently, so on the rare days that we have off, I try to teach my sister how to cook so she can eat different foods. Most of the time she just goes over to her friend's house. Poppy tries to stay up late so she can see me and mom more than just once in the morning, but most of the time I find her sleeping on the couch. I occasionally see my friends when I walk to Linda's, because I sometimes forget my lunch at home. They are usually coming out from Linda's or just passing by. Normally we give the friendly exchange of smiles, but today it was different.

Today I was rather upset with myself because I packed a really good lunch - leftover meatloaf. We made it last night because we were let out early due to a holiday. Days blur into the next, so I'm really not sure which holiday it was. My mom offered her lunch, but I declined because she needed a hardy meal more than I did. I made it to Linda's and grabbed a small tuna fish sandwich with a pack of crackers on the side. I made it to checkout and a very young woman started to check out my food- sliding it across the conveyer belt in a slow, methodical way. She wore big glasses that took up most of her face. She also didn't look much older than I was. Her face seemed very memorable at the time, but I can't recall much more about her. I do remember her saying, "So you like tuna? I've never been that big of a fan."

"Yeah it's pretty good but not as good as Spam."

"I agree."

I then paid her and started to leave the store. Just as I headed through the door, I heard someone call my name. I turned around, but nobody was there so I kept walking. I then heard my name again, but I couldn't see anyone. Finally, after a third time I looked across the street and Silvia were standing there. I could hardly recognize her because she had on a bright blue dress, her hair was curly, and she was modeling a new pair of glasses.

She ran across the street to walk with me. Normally I would have turned at Santon Street to get back to work, but I walked right past it because I knew a back route and Silvia was with me. She started with some small talk:

"How have you been?"

"I've been good. How about you?"

"I'm good."

Neither of us knew what to say so there was an awkward silence for a while. I restarted the conversation with:

"So, how's school going?"

"Good, good. I got moved up another grade. It's lonely without you because I don't have anyone to talk to at lunch. I miss you."

One thing about Silvia is she needs one person. What I mean is, at her house, her mom is her person. Because she is so shy, she doesn't get included in conversations much and people don't like repeating what they're saying. Her mom makes people include her and at school, and that's what I did. When I went to school, we would talk at lunch. Usually Silvia would come to lunch late because she has math right before lunch and that's on the other side of the school. By the time she sat down, all of us were normally in the middle of the conversation. Savana doesn't care to bring her up to speed on what we're talking about and because Susan and Sarah want to be Savana, they don't care either. I cared because I know how it feels to be left out. When she sat down, I would stop everyone from talking and I would give a condensed version of what we were talking about, this way she can have input on the conversation.

We continued our awkward conversation with fillers like, "the weather's nice" and ``That soap opera sounded cool last night." Eventually I couldn't take it anymore, I had to address the elephant in the room.

"Why did you change your look?"

She had a look on her face like she didn't know the question was coming.

"Savana said I needed to change so I did. We met at the end of the school day and she took me to some stores that I can shop from and she pointed out the stores not to go to. She helped me to pick out some dresses like the one I'm wearing. After we went to her house and she showed me how to curl my hair and put makeup on. Also, the glasses were a necessity which I received on my birthday."

I didn't really know how to reply because one of my best friends got turned into one of the popular girls; or at least she looked like one. I told her I needed to go so I said goodbye and wished her well, then I turned down Wallis Street and ran back to work because I was supposed to be back thirty minutes ago.

Day: August 1st

Year: 1945

Place: Earth

Time: Poppy's Birthday

It's the new year, and we have not received any good information. We've been able to help prevent some minor attacks but that's it. We haven't gotten very close to ending the war. The production of robots has consistently slowed down because we have numerous storage facilities filled with assembled bots. This allows us to go home earlier and spend more time with family. Poppy really likes that we are home earlier because she enjoys spending time with us. Even when we're home, my mom is constantly thinking about work. She worries a lot and I try to take her mind off of anything she's thinking, but it never works. She pretends to be fine, but I know whatever she's thinking about is slowly eating her up inside.

When we got home, Poppy came running up to me with the biggest smile I have seen on her face in a long time. She gave me a giant hug and dragged me into my room. Sitting in my room was a bunkbed. Poppy had made signs indicating that the bottom bunk was hers and the top was mine. Today was Poppy's 11th birthday. Instead of going shopping (because she did that for my birthday), I let her move into my room. She normally sleeps in my mom's room (we only have those two bedrooms). My mom has been awfully stressed lately so I thought that getting Poppy out of her room would make her less stressed and able to sleep better. I didn't mind because I knew she would be excited about it and all I want for her birthday is for her to be happy. Me and my mom aren't around much anymore, and I know that upsets her, so I wanted her to have the best birthday ever.

That night, I cooked dinner for everyone - Potato and Hot Dog salad for the main course and Jell-O salad for dessert. Those are some of Poppy's favorite foods so I knew she would like them. Mom didn't talk much during dinner, which kind of irritated me, but I didn't say anything. After dinner we played one of Poppy's favorite board games - The Game of Life. We, of course, let her win but we put up a good fight.

It was almost 11 o'clock and we all needed to get some sleep after celebrating all night. My mom went to her room and Poppy and I went to ours. Before we went to bed, I had to give Poppy her gift from me. I knew my mom bought her the bunkbed, so I had to get something to go with it. I saved up some of my money from work and bought her a sheet set with pillowcases. When I gave them to her, she opened them up so fast and put them on her bed. The sheets were a lavender purple with patches of a bright blue coloring. One of the pillowcases was baby pink outlined in baby blue and the middles looked like paint splatters in the color of bright purple. I could tell that she had the best birthday. We said goodnight to each other, and we went to sleep. I was happy with how my day went and I was just very happy in general.

Day: August 4th

Year: 1945

Place: Earth

Time: From Home to Work

This morning I was woken up by a loud bang in the kitchen. I jumped out of bed and rushed to see what it was. As I approached the kitchen, I heard an unfamiliar voice. I peeked over the doorway and there was one of the men in black cleaning up a bunch of pans on the floor. It looked as if he came through our kitchen window. About a minute later my mom rushed out of her room to see what all the ruckus was. Once she saw who is in the kitchen she walked in and started questioning why he was there. He didn't give a very thorough response. All he said was, "We need you two to come to the factory right now."

My mom and I rushed as fast as we could to get our uniform on and get something to eat. I made a piece of toast for my mom and one for me. I also wrote a note to my sister saying we had to get into work super early this morning. As we were driving to work, I could only wonder why they needed us so badly.

As we approached the warehouse, I noticed something strange. There were about twenty men dressed in black guarding the building, each holding something that I had never seen. We got out of the car near where the General was standing and were both practically yanked inside. The General especially had a hard grip on me. I could feel his nails giving way into my skin. I didn't know if it was because he thought I was going to slip away or if he just didn't realize how hard his grip was. He pulled us past all the workers who typically take early morning shifts because they have small children at home and their husbands are off to war. He pulled us past many of the men dressed in black, he even pulled us past our workstations. We had no clue where we were going. Finally, the General stopped in front of a door that had one guard on each side of it. The guard asked for ID so all three of us gave it. The door opened and a bunch of smoke came out. I could also tell that the door was suction sealed because of the loud noise it made when it opened. The door was very small, and we all had to hunch over to get through it, walking single file. The General entered first, followed by me, my mom, and then one of the men in black from the parking lot. To get to the inner room, we had to follow a series of tunnels. I could tell we were going farther and farther underground because the air was thin, and the walls/ceilings were made of dirt, mud, and concrete. It took a good while to get to a door, which looked strikingly similar to the other doors in the building. I began to think that this was a scam and the General just wanted to see if we would follow him. General Calcut told us that we needed to stay quiet because right above us is where everyone works, and everyone should be here by now. This made me wonder how long we had been walking for. He put in a password through the pad in the door and it opened. Once again it was pressure sealed. The room was very dark, and I couldn't see a lot other than a glowing screen. As we walked further into the room, the glowing screen grew bigger. Eventually, what I saw was truly amazing. There was an entire wall full of television screens, all looking at a different robot.

I couldn't figure out why the General wanted me and my mom here. Finally, he asked us to sit down in glass chairs, both of which were in front of the wall of television screens. He then proceeded to turn all of them off, except one. His screen said:

Henry Baker

1:20:06

General

I recognized the name. I had made that robot. It was an adult, but I made it when there was a shortage of parts for the children and we were waiting for the shipment to come in. The General picked up the remote and rewound the video. He eventually made it to a point where there were a lot of German Generals standing in a tent. The tent had a table in the middle with what looked like blueprints in it. I watched in horror as I realized that the blueprints were for a bomb. None of us could

figure out what the Germans were saying so General

Calcut brought in a translator. The General slipped

me a piece of paper to read. The paper said in

translated German,

"The Bomb to End the War."

Day: August 4th

Year: 1945

Place: Earth

Time: Moments Later

"The bomb to end the war! There must be some translation error. How did they figure out what they needed for such a good bomb?" I asked.

"There is no translation error. The German's are planning to create a bomb to end the war" said the General.

"But General they can't do that," I exclaimed.

"Yes, they can. Now I would like these two ladies escorted out of the room. You two can't tell another living soul about this. Additionally, I want someone who can draw an exact replica of those prints, so we have them. Also, I want the translator to come back and translate some of the conversation, so we know where they are planning on using this weapon," concluded the General.

None of us moved. We all looked at General Calcut in absolute horror. All we knew was that the Germans were making a bomb. We didn't know when it was going to be done, where they planned to strike first, and how many they were making. Once again, we were told to "GET GOING" so we left the room.

As we made our way upstairs, all I could think about was the fact that the Germans were making a bomb and we could do nothing about it. I didn't get very much work done that day. Ko-Ko and Benny could tell that there was something wrong with me, but I wasn't allowed to say anything.

When we made it home, I went straight to my room and mom went straight to hers. Poppy was spending the night at her friend's house, so we didn't have to worry about her. I spent about an hour sitting in my room just thinking. At that point, I started to smell something I had not smelled in quite a while. I left my room and went to the kitchen. There was my mom standing in front of the stove (like she used to) cooking up meatloaf and hot buttery mashed potatoes.

As she was cooking, it reminded me of when we didn't have to work, and I would come home from school to my mom standing in the kitchen cooking up some delicious treats. She would always ask how my day was, then she would ask how much homework I had because our favorite soap opera was going to be on the radio. Mom, Poppy, and I would all sit down to eat, and we would talk about the day. We would talk about our favorite parts of the day and our least favorite parts. There was a lot of laughing and smiling. We don't get that much anymore. I miss those moments.

I asked mom why she was cooking up such a good meal. She responded with,

"I felt like today you had such a hard day, so I wanted to make tonight special. I decided to cook up a nice meal, we could enjoy it in the living room while listening to a soap opera or two. Are you good with that?"

"I like that idea. Thanks, mom," I replied.

When we sat down to eat, I was happy and not stressed for once. We talked about all kinds of stuff, like how the General has such a funny voice. We cleaned up the kitchen and sat down to play a board game. I chose to play checkers because I dominate at that game. In the middle of game three -

I won all of them; not that it matters - we got a phone call. My mom had just run to the bathroom a few seconds earlier, so I picked up the phone.

"Hello?"

"Hello is this Dakota?"

"Yes, who is this?" I asked.

"It's General Calcut. We need you and your mom at work by 8:00 a.m. *sharp* tomorrow. We need to show you something."

He hung up the phone. That's how the conversation ended. No "Goodbyes" or "See you then." Just one man talking and hanging up. I put the phone down as my mom was coming out of the bathroom. She asked who it was, and I replied with, "General Calcut called telling us that we need to be there by 8:00 a.m. because he has something to show us."

Day: August 5th

Year: 1945

Place: Earth

Time: In the Factory

The next morning, we woke up very early and got to work as requested, all the while wondering what was so important. We were met at the front door by the General where he frantically took us to one of the main rooms. Sitting in the room were the three men in black, another individual that I had never seen before, and a translator. The unfamiliar person stood up and walked toward me. He shook my hand and told me that he specialized in making weapons. The General then mentioned that they had completed a copy of the blueprints for the bomb that the Germans were trying to make. They pulled me to the table where the blueprints were sitting. I had a knack for deciphering blueprints because I could envision what the end product might look. I took a look at the prints and I realized that this was an entirely new bomb that nobody in America had ever seen. After a few minutes of analyzing the prints, the General started talking. "Now that we have the prints, we need to start making this bomb! I'm transferring you and your mother from making robots to helping develop this bomb. You won't be working directly with it, but you will be helping to get all the pieces together. I feel that this bomb can help end the war, but we need to get the bomb done before the Germans do. Do you understand me?" he asked. "Yes, I understand," I replied.

He then continued to talk to me specifically. "I'm going to send you down to your old workspace and you're going to pick up any old papers or objects that you think you'll need for this project. Anything that has to do with creating a robot you're going to leave with Benny and Ko-Ko."

I didn't get a chance to reply because I was quickly escorted away. I packed up all of my things as quickly as I could, and right before I left, Ko-Ko said,

"Where are you going? We need you here!"

I couldn't respond to her because I wasn't allowed to say where or why I was going. So, I looked at her and I looked at Benny and I said to them both,

"Goodbye."

With that, I left not knowing when I was going to be able to return or if I was even going to return. Once I made it back to the room where General Calcut was, he told me that he had a special room set aside for this project. One of the men in black took me to the room. Not surprisingly, the room had black walls, a small desk, a small swivel chair, a bookshelf, and a television set in front of the room. On the screen of the television, I saw the name Henry Baker. I organized all of my stuff on the desk and lined up a few of my books on the bookshelf. As I was finishing up with the books, the General came in pushing a filing cabinet saying I would probably need it. He also informed me that the television I had in front of me was capable of watching any robot, not just the ones I made. A few hours later my mom came in to check on me. The General had also given her a room just like mine right next door.

She came to see if I wanted to eat lunch with her. We haven't been assigned an exact task to do yet, so I wasn't doing very much. I told her I would love to eat lunch with her. We both opened up our lunch boxes and realized that we forgot to pack lunches. We looked at each other and laughed. My mom grabbed her wallet and I grabbed mine, and we both walked down to Linda's to go get a sandwich. I decided to grab an egg salad sandwich and my mom got a tuna sandwich. We then left to go eat at the nearby park. We didn't have very much company because it was around midday, so most kids were at school and many people were at their jobs or across the sea at war. It was very calming, and it was nice to look over at my mom and see a giant smile across her face again. I didn't know the exact reason why she was smiling so much but I didn't really care. I was just happy she was smiling. And I was happy we were together.

After we finished eating, we went back to work and we sat at our desks for two more hours. Neither of us did anything in those two hours other than flip through the television watching what the robots saw. Eventually my mom asked the General if we could go home early because we weren't doing anything. He said yes and we left work. We didn't do much today, but I sure hope we get to do something helpful tomorrow.

Day: August 30th

Year: 1945

Place: Earth

Time: Weeks Later

A few weeks later, my life was totally different. All I do anymore is read blueprints and try to help in any way I can. By tomorrow our bomb should be completed. I have had to stay nights to work on this project. We are keeping a close eye on the Germans advancements. A time has been scheduled for tomorrow evening to test the bomb. If the test is successful, we can send it to Germany to hopefully end the war. I don't get much sleep anymore. I mostly run on 40-minute naps when I have the chance and chug coffee, which tastes horrible, but it gives me energy. I also get to go home on the weekends, so I get to catch up on some sleep then.

Mom gets more sleep than I do because I force her to go home and rest. She isn't doing too well. I hope the war will end soon so I can take care of her. She doesn't sleep much because she worries. She worries about me and Poppy, she worries about the war, and most of all she worries that this is her new life, that the war will never end, that our daily lives will be waking up, going to work, coming home late, and then repeating it again the next day. I feel I'm more optimistic about stuff related to the war. I try to show mom some of that optimism, but it doesn't really work.

Today I was sent home early (as in 5:30 p.m.) because I could barely keep my eyes open. Mom has already been home so when I walked in the house, she was surprised to see me. I was so tired I didn't eat dinner and I went right to my room. The strange thing was that I couldn't fall asleep. My mind was so active, and the fact that my eye bags had bags, didn't matter. All I could think about was how we needed the test tomorrow to go great otherwise we may not win the war. I looked at the small clock I had sitting on my desk to check the time. It was 7:30 p.m.! That doesn't seem insane to the average person, but I normally go to bed around 2:00 a.m.

Somehow my mom knew I was still up, so she came into my room with some warm milk and honey to help me sleep better. I wasn't concerned about waking up Poppy because when she falls asleep nothing can wake her. I once tested it. I got a metal pot and a spoon and started banging them together. The only response I got was some mumbling about a dream she was having. Mom wasn't too pleased about that, but I let her know it was all "For science." I thought about that memory while sitting there with my mom. I sometimes miss the good times when we could do things like that.

After I finished my warm milk and honey, mom left the room and I fell right to sleep. Nothing about tomorrow even crossed my mind.

The next morning came surprisingly quickly. I was working on a full night's sleep and ready to conquer the day. Unbelievably, for the first five minutes of the day I even forgot that today was bomb testing day. Then I remembered and could barely stand. I remember wishing that I could see into the future and be prepared for what lay ahead. The morning dragged on for what seemed like an eternity until we received the announcement that the bomb was completed, and we could test early. I got butterflies in my stomach and could not stop thinking about the bad things that could happen. We were all escorted into black cars and drove for two hours into the middle of nowhere so we could detonate the bomb. In the field where we finally stopped, there was a bunker that we all had to file in. In total there were 10 of us and we all could tell that someone had an onion for lunch. All of us were given poison gas masks just in case. We were just far enough away so nothing bad could come to us. A man in black was designated to bring the bomb to the field. Where the bomb laid, there was a camera so we could see the bomb and make sure everything was ready. I was handed a clipboard with a long list on it. Once everyone was settled the countdown started.

"10"

I could barely breathe.

"9"

My hands were shaking in fear.

"8"

I was sweating bullets.

"7"

There was so much tension in the room.

"6"

We were told to get our masks on if they weren't on already.

"5"

It was silent in the room.

"4"

There was so much that could go wrong.

"3"

Almost there.

"2"

My heart was pounding.

"1"

"BOOM"

The bomb was detonated. The noise was loud. You could hear scribbles on everyone's paper. I looked down on my check list.

#1-BOMB WENT OFF SUCCESSFULLY

That was a check.

#2-EVERYONE WAS FAR ENOUGH AWAY

That was a check too. I went through the entire list. All were checks. Everyone had all checks. This was such a relief. Everyone started cheering and screaming. We created a bomb in a few weeks that the Germans needed more time to complete. Everything was perfect. The U.S. did it. All that was left to do was to use it to win the war. We were told that we could take tomorrow off to rest and prepare for Monday when we were to plan out our strategy on when and where to use our new weapon. I was elated it worked and was looking forward to more sleep.

Day: August 31st

Year: 1945

Place: Earth

Time: The Next Day

I woke up late today and was rushing to work. General Calcut told me that I needed to come into work early today. Just me, not my mom. Typically, when I have to go into work early, mom has to come with, so she wakes me up. That didn't happen today, and I woke up very late. I quickly got into my work clothes and sprinted out the door. On the way to work I stopped into Linda's because I was starving! I grabbed some cream cheese and a bagel and left.

I made it to work with two minutes to spare. After I quickly flashed my ID, I went inside, and the entire place looked different. There were tarps covering the floor and sheets hung up to cover bulletin boards filled with a ton of papers. I slowly walked to my desk, trying to figure out what happened. When I got to my desk there was a note on my desk that read,

"Go to the General's office. He will be expecting you!"

I set my bag down and went to his office. As the note said, he was sitting there patiently awaiting my arrival. In front of him he had at least ten papers lined in two rows of five. I sat directly across from him and I couldn't help but wonder if I was being fired. He looked at me and said, "I'm glad you're here. We needed someone whom we trusted to come in and sit with us, and chat."

My heart started beating faster.

"Please, come over here. We want you to look at these papers," General Calcut ordered.

I walked over to the papers and I couldn't believe what I was seeing. On those papers there were pictures of Germany, there were letters, and there were pictures of Nazi's. There was one paper that I couldn't figure out what it was. As I was trying to take a closer look at it, General Calcut took it away. He started to read it.

"On September 2nd of 1945, both Germany and Japan will be bombed with the new bomb that we successfully created."

September 2nd was just two days away. I didn't realize that we were going to use this so soon after the test. I asked why so soon, and the General replied, "We need to bomb before the Germans do."

We continued to talk about the plan and the basics I would have to know. At some point while we were talking, one man in black barged into the room. He said he had an urgent message for the General. As he said this, he had a certain tone in his voice implying that he wanted me to leave, but the General put his hand on my shoulder giving me the idea that he wanted me to stay. When the man in black realized that the General was comfortable with me staying, he went over and asked General Calcut a few questions in private. I knew they were about me, but I chose not to say anything. The man in black took a step closer to the door as if he was getting ready to run out when he said, "We were watching the robots as we were instructed to do, and the translator gasped and started running around the room frantically. He was muttering something under his breath that none of us could quite decipher. Then out of nowhere he said, "the Germans have finished their bomb and are planning to use it tomorrow!'"

General Calcut immediately ran into a different room. I followed him to see if I could help with anything. When I walked in, he was ruffling through a bunch of papers and he was doing a lot of calculations. He then left this room just as quickly as he arrived. He went back to his office and then left again. He did this back and forth for about 10 minutes until finally he scribbled something down on a piece of paper and handed it to me. He told me to run it right down to level 4B - which happened to be the lowest level in the building. He also told me to do this quickly because he needed an answer right away.

I ran as fast as my little legs could take me. I contemplated looking at what the note said, but I chose not to. After finding my way down to level 4B, I quickly went into the reception office and gave the note to the lady sitting behind the desk. She opened the note and immediately ran to a different room to deliver the note. I watched as everybody had the same reaction. They all jumped a little and then ran to a different room. Finally, after a few minutes, I got a new note that I had to bring to the General.

I ran back up to the top level where General Calcut was. After delivering that letter to him, he paused for a moment, and then indicated that he had made a decision. He pulled me into a room and told me that the plans had changed, and we needed to use our bomb today.

Day: August 31st

Year: 1945

Place: Earth

Time: Minutes Later

"Today? Don't you think that's a little early since we just tested it?" I asked.

"There is no other option. We have to do it today or it'll never get done. I need you to spread the news and tell everybody to be here by 12 p.m. Go!" exclaimed General Calcut.

Before I left, I was given a list of each person that needed to come to work, as well as their addresses. We weren't going to tell the world quite yet, but we knew we needed to today at some point.

The first stop on my list was Amy Jenkins. She was around my mom's age and she helped with calculations. She doesn't always come into work

117

because she's not always needed since we have all calculations down for the robots. When I told her the news, she kind of freaked out like I expected her to, but I had to get out of there quickly because I had a bunch more people on my list. I wish I could have stayed and told her all the details, but I knew that wasn't a part of my job.

Next stop was Marion Heart. She was about 20-years-old but extremely smart and so that's why they recruited her to the factory. After I told her, she seemed calmer than Amy Jenkins, so I was able to leave her house faster.

I got through a bunch of people and they each had different reactions to the news. After my entire list I went to the one person I was dreading to go to... my mom. I don't know why I didn't want to go to her, but I think now, looking back, it was because I did not want to make her life any more stressful than it already was.

I went into the house and my mom was surprised to see me. Both of us expected me to be there way longer than I had been. I brought my mom to the living room and sat her down on the couch. I told her I was here for a reason and she needed to listen. She had a very concerned look on her face, but I knew I just had to rip off the bandage. I looked her right in the eyes and told her, "Based on information we received today, we have to drop the bomb this afternoon."

After I said that she turned very pale and said she needed to go lie down. I brought her a glass of water. I told her that I needed to go back to the factory and if she needed anything at all to please call me. I felt bad leaving her, but I knew I had to.

I made it back to the factory and told General Calcut that everyone had been informed of the news. He brought me into a room where he wanted me to fill out different pieces of paper that all had a bunch of random questions on them. One of the questions asked if I thought the bomb was ready to be used today. Another asked if I thought this was a good idea. All of the questions have the same general theme, but I knew they were all necessary.

After completing the questionnaire, I was told to return to General Calcut's office because he needed me immediately. He told me that he had designed a flyer that would inform all the others about using the bomb. He needed me to make some copies of the flyer. Truth be told, I had never used the copy machine before, mostly because I never needed to, and it was only invented a few years ago.

I copied about 100 papers and brought them straight to General Calcut. He looked at the copies and told me to go start hanging them up around town. It might not seem like something to be nervous about, but I was very nervous because I didn't know how the general public was going to react. I also didn't know how they were going to react to a 13-year-old girl hanging up the flyers.

I started in my neighborhood. One of my neighbors, Mr. Heatherwood, was sitting on his porch when I was hanging up a flyer. Mr. Heatherwood was not able to fight in this war due to injuries he received during the first world war. After I hung that flyer and walked away, I watched as he got up from his porch and pulled the flyer off of the pole where it was nailed. I watched as utter shock fell across his face. I wish I could explain but I had

121

no time to. He was not the only person with that reaction - just the first. After I hung the last flyer, I rushed back to the warehouse. I looked at my watch. It was exactly 11:17 a.m. I knew in a little over an hour we were going to drop a bomb that could end the war.

Day: August 31st

Year: 1945

Place: Earth

Time: Later that Day

12:18, 19, 20. The minutes kept passing. All of us waiting to be told what to do. Even I wasn't informed what was going to happen next. 12:24, 25, 26, 27. I watched the clock anxiously waiting to be called into a different room, waiting to be told what to do, waiting. There was small chatter throughout the room. People were talking about how they were not sure this is going to work, people wondering about their families, people concerned about what the public will think. I felt that I was the least concerned out of everybody because I had the most information. I've never felt so sure that something is going to work in my entire life. 12:34, 35, 36. Time, still ticking. Finally, at 12:42:06, General Calcut barged in the room and asked everybody to stand in a single-file line. I originally started in the middle of the line but was quickly relocated to the front. Behind me were Benny and Ko-Ko. We were told that we were in front because they wanted to make sure the kids were safe - but I truly knew they wanted me specifically in front, they just had to make a believable story.

The tension in the building was rising. We were all brought into a very big room that had a medium sized television in the middle of it. There were only enough chairs for 6 people, and everybody else had to stand around the room. The television flickered on and we saw a sky view from the plane carrying one of the bombs to Germany. Because we were all focused on the television none of us realized that a second television was wheeled into the room. On the second television there was a sky view to the plane that carried the second bomb going to Japan. We watched as the plane that headed to Germany slowly grew closer and closer to land. We watched as the plane started slowing down. We listened to the pilots of the plane as they we're making sure they were in the right spot. We watched the camera shift so we could see the bomb being dropped. The countdown began 10, 9, 8, 7, 6, 5, 4, 3, 2.

This was at the moment we had been waiting for.

.... 1.

Everyone watched as the bomb was dropped from the plane. We watched as it fell through the sky cutting through clouds. We heard the whooshing sound as it fell. The room? Silent. All of us knew

125

that we would not see much of the explosion because the plane had to get away quick enough to not be destroyed. We watched the screen and it finally happened. The explosion.

A giant muffin shaped cloud colored red, orange, and yellow showed up on the screen instantly. Dust everywhere. We could see the shockwave. The plane had to fly away so we couldn't see much more of it, but we knew that was that. Germany had to surrender. The room fell silent. The mood was somber.

After the first explosion, the television was wheeled out of the room so we could all focus on the next one. Everything that happened with the German bomb was mirrored by the Japanese bomb. The talking of the pilots, the cutting through the sky, the whooshing as the bomb fell, the muffin shaped explosion, the flying away. I couldn't imagine how much this affected people and families. I knew if I kept thinking about that I could never live with myself knowing I helped to make that monstrosity happen.

After the second television was finally wheeled off, the lights were turned back on and everyone just looked at each other. We all put our heads down in silence for all the people affected by both of those bombs. After that, we all went to Linda's to buy some York Peppermint Patties to take our minds off of what we had just witnessed.

Because it was such an eventful day, General Calcut let us take the rest of the day off. I planned on spending my day sleeping because I was exhausted. I went home and made some jellied chicken for Poppy and me. It tasted delicious, one of my favorite meals.

Right before I was about to go to bed, I got a call from General Calcut. He said he wanted to personally inform me that the war was officially... OVER! Both Japan and Germany surrendered. I didn't know what to say because I was in complete and utter shock. I knew we could do it, but I didn't know it would happen this fast. General Calcut wanted to inform me that I was the first person other than him, and the men in black to hear this great news. I know it seems like a lot of people already knew, but it made me feel very special to know that I was the first of the workers to be told. I was also told that the only people that I could actually tell about this was my mom and my sister. General Calcut made it very clear that I couldn't tell my sister how I knew the information, but he did grant me permission to tell her which made me very happy.

By the time I heard this news my mom was already asleep, but I knew I couldn't wait till morning to tell her, so I went to a room and woke her up telling her I had urgent news. Poppy was still awake, so I just told her to meet me in the living room. I told them both the news and just as General Calcut expected, Poppy asked how I knew. I told her it was classified, and she wasn't allowed to know. She kind of got mad at me for that response but I didn't care, the war was over. I didn't have to worry about one of my robots malfunctioning or if I made one wrong and it broke down.

I was also told by General Calcut that my mom and I still had to show up for work tomorrow, but it might be one of our last days. He told me that he planned on telling everybody else in the factory and we had to figure out how to tell the public if they hadn't already heard. They certainly heard by the morning.

I thought that this was one of the best moments of my life. I had nothing else to worry about. I could go back to school, spend time with my family, and get to see my mom every night as we talked over a fully cooked meal on the table. Looking back, I couldn't have been so far from the truth.

Day: October 3rd

Year: 1949

Place: Earth

Time: Years Later

The war's been over for a few years now and life has not yet returned to normal as I expected. About a year after the war ended, my mom was asked to help with a different project for the government. They said it was too advanced for me but if they needed help, they knew the right person to go. It turns out that in all the chaos of making the robots and making sure that they were made correctly, we forgot to make a shutdown button that was not on the robot. For this reason, we are not allowed to search for them and deactivate them.

The robots are programmed to act like humans. Somehow, in all the confusion of trying to figure out how to shut them down, all the bots stored in the U.S. were turned on and now live amongst humans.

But they are taking over all aspects of life. Soon there will be nothing for real humans to do. Because they were designed so well, it's very difficult for the average human to decipher a robot from their best friend. I say average person because people like me, as in those people who created the robots, know how to tell the difference.

We were able to shut down the cameras in them, but we have yet to find a way to shut them down completely. They are taking over the world. This is not good.

The assignment that my mom is working on is to help make flight pods that could fit thousands of people. The goal is to use these pods to get people off of Earth and move them to Mars. We have no other choice but to leave the planet. The robots have officially taken over. You go into a supermarket and a robot is working there, you go to the gas station and a robot is working there, people are starting to sell houses to robots. Nobody can tell the difference, so they don't know who to give jobs to and who not to. This is creating an extreme shortage of jobs for actual human beings. Because they are robots, they are designed to learn fast and excel at everything they learn how to do. Once the robot learns how to do the job, they learn how to perfect it and master it. This means business owners have no need to hire anyone else. One example of this was my friend's mom. She got let go from her job just a few days ago because a robot could do her job better. She was at that job for seventeen years.

The hard part about this entire situation is that there were thousands of robots made and only fifteen people, including me, know the difference between humans and robots.

I don't know very many specifics about the pods because I'm not on that project, but I do know that my mom has been working day and night. I never went back to school because I needed to take care of Poppy and my mom. My mom doesn't have time to make meals anymore. I make sure she eats breakfast every morning and I always pack her lunch, so she has one for the day. She could have always run down to Linda's and bought lunch, but I knew without me she would never go.

I always have dinner prepared for when she comes home. Poppy came home a few hours earlier, so I didn't have to have dinner ready yet. I do always make her an afternoon snack though. I make sure we all eat as a family at the dinner table and I make everybody talk about their days. My mom and I came up with a fake job that she has to go to everyday because Poppy still isn't allowed to know about any jobs that have to do with the government.

After dinner my mom generally goes to her room to work. Around 9:00 - 9:15 at night, I make her come out of her room and take a break. Sometimes she takes longer breaks and sometimes she tells me she has too much work and never actually would come out. Because of this task from the government, mom has not been as much of a mother figure like she used to be. I took over that position to make sure that everybody is okay - which is fine by me.

At this point, I thought the government had given up on trying to find a way to shut down the robots because they spent all of their time and energy creating these pods. I don't know when they will be complete, but I'm hoping it is soon because I know I couldn't spend the rest of my life trying to explain to people how to decipher robots and humans. I also didn't want to have a job later in life where I'm working side-by-side with a robot.

As I had explained before I don't know much about the pods progress or much about them in general, but one thing I had heard from my mom was that the U.S. is not the only country trying to get their people off of Earth. I had a conversation with my mom a long time ago about what the government was planning on doing. I don't remember very much of it, but I do remember something about different planets and how the U.S. claimed Mars. I also remember something about countries working together to get off of Earth. The conversation we had went on for a few hours, but I don't remember much of it because it happened a few years ago. Yes, these pods have been in development for a few years. The pods were estimated to take longer to make than the robots, but I highly doubt that with the amount of new technology we had.

There are many things I wish I could have told myself around that time. I wish I could have told myself the pods were not that amazing and that I would have to get used to living with robots.

Day: October 7th

Year: 1949

Place: Earth

Time: Jackson Street

While I was sitting at the kitchen table eating my lunch, I heard a man yelling outside. I went outside to see what the commotion was about. He was yelling, "Important news! Everyone must go to the back of the field of Jackson Street for an unveiling. Bring everything you love. More information on the posters hung around town." He then walked away yelling the phrase over and over. I left the house looking for one of the flyers. I read it as soon as I found one.

The flyer read:

"Go to the back of Jackson street with everything you love at approximately 2:00 p.m. _Sharp._"

I had a sneaky suspicion I knew what it meant but I could have been wrong.

My mom came home at about 1:30 p.m. telling me to pack my clothes and grab things I could not live without. I asked her if my guess was right and she confirmed my hunch. The pods were ready to launch. We would be able to finally leave. She also told me that the U.S. was not the only country ready, so it wasn't going to be that monumental of a moment.

I packed my clothes, toothbrush, hairbrush, and anything else I thought I needed. I also put on my favorite bracelet that my mom got me when I was 5 years old. It has a charm on it that looks like a unicorn. I always felt like it brought me luck. I was ready to leave this robot infested planet.

At about 1:50 p.m., my mom, sister, and I left the house. When we arrived at the field, there were five pods lined up ready for take-off. There were also a lot of people looking on in amazement. They didn't know what these things were and why they were sitting there. Even though I knew what they were I had never seen one, so I was also in awe as I gazed at them. They could hold thousands of people at a time.

All the pods looked exactly alike except for the number on the outside, each painted with an all-white base. There was a printed American flag encircling the entirety of the middle section. The flag also had a golden border. Right above that, a number represented the identity of the pod – 1 through 5.

At exactly 2:00 p.m., General Calcut walked in front of everyone to speak. He was holding a blue megaphone in his right hand. He started by saying,

"I know everyone is probably wondering what these five big things are that are sitting in front of you. These are called pods. These pods will bring us from this robot infested Earth to Mars. I know that might seem like a shock to most of you, but it is the only way to escape. If we don't do this now, we may never know what the difference between a robot is and what a human is. Now, the men in black that are standing near the pods will call out names. If your name is called you will go up to the lovely lady sitting at the table over there and she will instruct you as to which pod that you should go to, as well as your seat number. A reminder it will be cramped in there and if we underestimated the amount of people, some may have to stand which is fine because we do have railings on the inside walls. We also have a few extra seats but those will only be used for women with infants. Okay, start loading people on. Remember this is for the best!"

With that, he walked away and the men in black started to shout out names.

"Wallis Mel Fort…"

"Sarah Lee Silver..."

"Emmaline Rose Utter…"

I knew Emmaline. She constantly bragged about how her family hunted otters in the 1800s.

I patiently waited for my name to be called. Poppy's was called way before mine. I didn't understand why they didn't go by family, but it wasn't my system to follow.

"Michael Todd Farris…"

"Gavin Lax Zander…"

My mom was called but I still waited.

"Regina Marie Harrison…"

"Tib San Zeltar…"

Finally, after waiting for what felt like an eternity, I heard my name called. I went over to the table and the lady looked at me. She smiled and looked for my name on the list. She knew me so I didn't have to give her my name. She was my old math teacher. She never liked me because I would always correct her when she was wrong, and I would sometimes do her job by going around and helping the other students who were struggling. She told me I was in pod 5, the last pod. She also mentioned that I had a special spot and that I had to go to the man in black standing near pod 5.

Walking over toward pod 5, I could still hear the names being called out. I felt a sense of relief upon hearing my co-worker Benny's name being called, and not much longer after that, Ko-Ko.

As I approached the man in black and gave him my name. He brought me into the pod and sat me up in the front in a seat that had a sign noting the seat was "Reserved." The seat also listed my name. I felt so special. Both my mom and sister were sitting next to me.

Poppy did *not* seem overly thrilled. She complained the entire way here about how she didn't want to leave Earth and all her friends. She also wasn't the happiest when she learned she had to pack the bare essentials in 20 minutes. When we got into the pod, she still wasn't too happy, so I tried to comfort her and tried to make her laugh. I told some of my best jokes and she didn't laugh very much. I got maybe a snicker or two, but I could tell she wasn't going for it because she was just trying to give me the cold shoulder. All she said was that she missed her boyfriend Henry and how she wished she was with him. I would also like to mention that she blamed this whole thing on mom and me because we helped to create the robots that we now have to flee from. I couldn't handle this attitude anymore. I snapped. I told her that Henry doesn't matter right now and that we are lucky to be sitting where we were because we were way less crammed and we got special treatment. I also told her that if it wasn't for those robots, The World War II might still be going on. She rolled her eyes and made a weird grunting noise. Then she asked the person next to her to switch seats. My mom held Poppy's shoulder and apologized to the person sitting next to Poppy for her behavior. She then followed that with a lecture about appropriate behavior. I bet it would have gone on longer if General Calcut didn't enter our pod. He told us to look at the screen at the front of the pod in a few moments because it would be telling us everything we needed to know.

We all patiently waited for the screen. I asked one of the men in black if there was any food on the pod. He pulled me up out of my seat very quickly and brought me to the back of the pod (where nobody could see us) and opened a door that was loaded with snacks. He told me to pick out whatever I wanted and if anyone asks, I brought them from home. I picked out Chex Party Mix, a Skybar, and M&Ms. I brought the snacks back to my seat and shared them with my family. After some food in her, Poppy seemed a little less grouchy.

After a couple of more minutes, the screen finally turned on. General Calcut's face popped up and he immediately jumped right into the procedures:

"First things first, everything is situated and ready. Everyone should have a safety belt on that should be clicked in. if it's not please do so now. Next, I would like everyone to look under their seats to check to make sure they have a Parachute, an Oxygen Mask, and an alert button. If you are missing one of these please inform one of the men in black what you are missing and tell them your seat number, so they know who to give the item to. The alert button will vibrate in case of an emergency. If this does happen, we will have an announcement over the speaker phone directing you what to do. In case of an emergency related to a fellow passenger, contact one of the men in black. Bathrooms will be located on the left-hand area of the pod. Finally, the doors will be closing soon. When they do, it will take a minute to get the lights up and running so it may be a little dark at first. Also, we will be broadcasting the pod doors closing so people know that if their loved ones are in a different pod, they will be safe. Please stay calm, safe and enjoy the ride."

His picture clicked off the screen and chatter started back up again.

Less than two minutes later the screen turned back on. You could see all the pods lined up. You saw the door closing on pod one, then pod two, then three, then four. All of those went smoothly. Then

148

came our pod- it wouldn't close. The mechanism wasn't working.

General Calcut came running into our pod, seemingly coming directly toward me. He crouched down beside me and told me everything that was potentially wrong, and he asked if I had any ideas on how to fix this. My mind had one answer and one answer only. I asked, "Is there any way to close the pod from the outside?"

"Yes, one way! There is a lever that can be pulled! Brilliant idea!"

We brainstormed ideas on how to get the person pulling the lever back into the pod. We knew that a person had to be in this pod because the other pods were already closed and about to take off. Finally, we came up with the idea that the person would be tied to a rope, pull the lever, and be yanked quickly into the pod. We went through so many ideas, but this was the only one that could potentially work.

General Calcut got up in front of the Pod and told everyone the plan. There were a lot of gasps and a few people screamed. People were scared. General Calcut asked the final question, "Who is willing to go pull the lever?"

Nobody moved. It was silent. Once again, the question was asked.

"Who is willing to go pull the lever?"

It was so silent you could hear a pin drop. Finally, after minutes of waiting, someone stood up…...I did.

"I will pull the lever," I bravely said.

Day: October 7th

Year: 1949

Place: Earth

Time: On the Pod Behind Jackson Street

"No, I want somebody else, preferably an adult," said General Calcut.

"I will go. I think I'm perfect for this. You need someone to leave the pod and to be pulled back by the rope. I'm light weight which means it should be easy to pull me in. There is no question here. I am doing this," I argued.

"Fine. You know this is the right thing to do," conceded General Calcut.

I got up out of my seat and everyone started to cheer and applaud. My mom was screaming and crying. She tried to pull me back to my seat, but I told her I needed to do this. She had to be restrained by some of the men in black, otherwise, I may have never gone through with this. Before I left, I saw a hint of worry in Poppy's face and I also saw her start to cry. I assumed she was thinking about all the good times we had playing games, telling stories, eating breakfast together, and moving in my room together. I could tell she was scared and that she didn't want me to go.

I was escorted to the door where the rope was sitting. As I was being tied up, I was told to quickly pull the lever, and then to look back so that I could be pulled back in. I told them I understood as they tightened the rope. I watched as the other end of the rope was tied to the bar that was around the walls. I was approached by General Calcut. He crouched down next to me and looked me dead in the eyes and said, "You have a good heart, kid. Just know I thought of you as one of my own. I was surprised by you. I knew that you were smart, but I never knew that you would be one of the smartest people I would ever meet. Your bravery is something to be proud of. You surprised me on many levels, and you were always there when I needed someone to do any job for me, whether it was getting coffee or crunch some numbers. You were the best that ever happened to the government. You will be written into history books, kid. I hope you know that by you doing this, you will become a hero."

With that he gave me a big hug and wished me luck.

I made it to the end of the big door ready to jump. I looked back behind me and I saw my mom in tears, General Calcut giving me the thumbs up, the rope tied to the bar. I knew I was ready. Right before I jumped off, a single tear rolled down my cheek. That tear inched down my face, navigating through a jungle of freckles.

I then did what I was instructed to do - I jumped. That tear stood still on my face, not moving until I hit the ground. The tear then fell to the ground making a mark on the reddish brownish dirt.

I walked over to the command center. It looked deserted in there. Chairs on the ground, dust on the controls, mice scurrying on the floor. I found the lever and my heart started to race like the cars racing in NASCAR. There was a glass case surrounding the lever. As I lifted it off, a dust cloud enveloped my face. This caused me to drop the glass which shattered into a million pieces. I looked at the lever for a good minute. The circular red topper was chipped, showing the wood underneath, the stained wood base was also horribly blotchy. I put my hand on the lever. It rested there until I built up enough courage to pull it. I started to count down, 3, 2, 1. I didn't pull it. I couldn't. I was too afra……. I pulled it.

I ran out of there as quickly as possible. I watched as the door started to close. I ran out as though I was being chased by a lion. I needed to get back in range - close enough to be pulled back in. As I started to be pulled up, I realized I was never going to make it. The door was going to be shut before I even had a chance. I tried so hard, but I couldn't make it. I slowly started to untie the knot from my waist. My hands trembled. A river streaming down my face, each freckle a pebble in the river. I got the first knot out, then the second. All I had to do was to step out. I thought about my family and stepped out of the rope and dropped it to the floor. I watched the rope get closed into the door. The rope didn't make it.

I fell to the ground sobbing. My hands were still trembling. My heart was aching. I clutched the bracelet in both of my hands.

As the pod flew off, I thought I could hear my mom screaming in pain. All I could think about was when I was little and I started to get upset, my mom would bring me to the couch and cuddle and sing me my favorite song called Hush Little Baby by Graeme Revell. We would sit there, and she would sing that song over and over until I felt better. As I got older, I would sing that song to Poppy when she felt upset. As I sat in the dirt sobbing, I sang myself that song to ease the pain.

After some time, I gathered myself together and walked back home feeling alone and not knowing what to do with myself. I first went to my mom's room and laid in her bed. I thought about the fact that she was sleeping here just a few hours ago and how she's on her way to Mars. I eventually cried myself to sleep knowing I would never wake up to a full house again. Never wake up to see my Mom or Poppy ever again.

Made in the USA
Monee, IL
08 April 2021